Magic
Animal Friends

For Lily Grace Mutter

Special thanks to Valerie Wilding

ISBN 978-0-545-90743-9

10 9 8 7 6 5 4 3 2 1   16 17 18 19 20

Printed in the U.S.A.   40
First printing 2016

Emily Prickleback's Clever Idea

Daisy Meadows

Scholastic Inc.

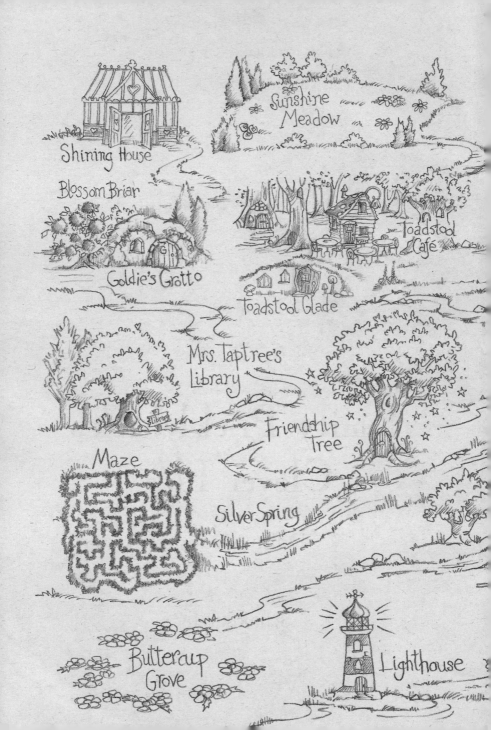

Shining House

Sunshine Meadow

Blossom Briar

Goldie's Grotto

Toadstool Café

Toadstool Glade

Mrs. Taptree's Library

Friendship Tree

Maze

Silver Spring

Buttercup Grove

Lighthouse

Map of Friendship Forest

Ace Air Travel

Windmill

Mr. Cleverfeather's Inventing Shed

Muddlepups' Den

Treasure Tree

Sparkly Falls

Featherbills' Barge

Waterwheel

Entrance to the Caverns

Swamp

Grizelda's Tower

Can you keep a secret? I thought you could!

Then I'll tell you about an enchanted wood.

It lies through the door in the old oak tree.

Let's go there now—just follow me!

We'll find adventure that never ends,

And meet the Magic Animal Friends!

Love,
Goldie the Cat

Contents

CHAPTER ONE

Gold in the Mist

Lily Hart put the box she was carrying gently down on the table. "This is my favorite part," she said, tucking her short, dark hair behind her ears.

Her best friend, Jess Forester, stood next to her. It was an early Saturday morning, and the misty air was making her blond

hair even curlier than usual. "It's one of the best things about Helping Paw," she said. "Sending animals home when they're better!"

Lily nodded. She felt so lucky that her parents ran the Helping Paw Wildlife Hospital in a barn near their house. She and Jess both adored animals and helped out there whenever they could. She carefully opened the box and smiled at the cute little hedgehog curled up inside. The hedgehog's leg had been hurt, so its owner had brought it to Helping Paw.

Now that its leg was better, it was time
for the hedgehog to go home.

Lily picked up the hedgehog and
brought it over to its owner.

"Oh, Snicklefritz, I missed you!" the

young woman said. "Thanks, girls!" She
cuddled the hedgehog closely and then
went over to talk with Mr. Hart.

As Jess watched, something else caught
her eye . . . a flash of gold.

"Look, Lily!" she exclaimed. "Did you
see that?"

"What?" asked Lily.

Jess peered through the mist. "I'm sure I
saw golden fur," she said.

Lily felt a shiver of excitement. "Do you
think it's Goldie?"

Goldie was a beautiful green-eyed cat,
and the girls' special friend. She had taken

them on lots of adventures in Friendship
Forest, a magical world where the
most amazing thing happened—all
the animals talked!

"Yes, there she is!" cried Lily. Both girls
ran to the tall clump of rushes that grew
beside Brightley Stream. They stroked
the golden cat while she purred happily,
rubbing against their legs.

"I wish you could talk in our world,
Goldie," said Lily. "I wonder if Friendship
Forest needs help again!"

A horrible witch called Grizelda
wanted to drive the animals out of the

forest so she could have it all to herself.
Friendship Forest was full of beautiful
trees and flowers, with the animals'
beautiful homes dotted among them.
Grizelda wanted to turn it into a dark,
gloomy place that only a witch would
like. The girls and Goldie had managed
to stop her evil plans so far, but now
Grizelda had new magical helpers—
dragons!

With a swish of her tail, Goldie
bounded toward the stepping stones and
crossed into Brightley Meadow.

Lily and Jess followed her to the lifeless

6

oak

tree that

stood in the

middle of the misty

meadow. They knew

what was going to

happen next!

As Goldie

reached the tree,

it was suddenly

bathed in sunlight.

Leaves sprang from the branches and

bright-yellow flowers blossomed in the

grass below. Butterflies and bees appeared
from nowhere and beautiful birdsong
echoed all around.

"It's so exciting when the tree comes
to life," Jess squealed, as letters appeared,
carved into the broad trunk. Jess and
Lily held hands and read them together.
"Friendship Forest!"

As they spoke, a little door with a
leaf-shaped handle appeared in the trunk.

Jess opened it and Goldie darted into the golden glow that shone inside.

The girls followed her through the door and into the shimmering light. They felt a tingly feeling all over. Lily squeezed Jess's arm happily, knowing that the tingle meant they were shrinking, just a little bit.

As the golden glow faded, the girls found themselves in a beautiful clearing surrounded by tall trees. Tiny cottages nestled among tree roots, and the warm air was filled with the scent of flowers. They were back in Friendship Forest! And in front of them, standing up with

a golden scarf around her neck, was
Goldie.

"Hello, girls," she said.

"Finally we can talk to you!" cried
Lily, as both girls hugged her.

"It's wonderful to be back in the
forest," said Jess. "But is everything okay?
Is Grizelda causing trouble?"

Goldie shook her head. "Everything is
fine! I brought you here so I could take
you to see something special."

"Ooh, what?" asked Jess excitedly.

"The Rushy River Race!" Goldie cried.

CHAPTER TWO

The Waterwheel

"A boat race!" said Lily. "I can't wait!"

Goldie bent down to pick up a basket
that was tucked in the roots of the
Friendship Tree. "I've got another surprise
for you!" she said with a smile. She
opened the lid and the girls peeked inside.

"Mmmm! Blossom buns and watercress sandwiches!" said Lily.

"Cherry bread!" said Jess. "And bottles of strawberry soda—yum!"

"Everyone who goes to the Rushy River Race takes a picnic to share with their friends," Goldie said, shutting the lid.

Lily and Jess grinned at each other. Going to Friendship Forest was always exciting, but coming for a race and a picnic sounded even better!

"The race is at Willowtree River," Goldie continued as they walked. "Do you remember our adventure there?"

"Yes, that was when we rescued little Ellie Featherbill," said Lily, smiling at the thought of the adorable duckling. Maybe they'd see her again today!

As they wandered through Toadstool Glade, Molly Twinkletail the mouse waved to them from the Toadstool Café. "Hello!" she called from the window. The little mouse was sitting inside, eating toffee toast with her mole friend, Lola Velvetnose.

"Hello, Molly!" said Jess and Lily.

Lola's little pink nose went *woffle woffle* as she sniffed to discover who Molly was talking to. "I smell honey," she said, peering through her round purple-framed glasses. "It's Jess!"

Lily laughed. "Lola always says you smell like honey, Jess," she said.

Lola's nose went *woffle woffle* again. "And that must be you, Lily," she said. "You smell like strawberries."

"Thank you, Lola!"

Lily said, laughing. "Are you coming to the Rushy River Race?"

"As soon as we've finished our toffee toast," said Molly. "I'm so excited!"

Jess, Lily, and Goldie set off again, passing other animals on their way to the river. Some carried picnic baskets, some had blankets or umbrellas, and everyone was chattering happily.

"What a beautiful day!" said Lily.

"The Shining House makes sure it's always sunny and warm here," Jess remembered happily.

"Thanks to you two," added Goldie.

The Shining House was cared for by the Flufftail squirrel family, who kept its magic working so that warm, bright sunlight always shone beneath the trees.

But recently, Chilly, Grizelda's ice dragon, had put a spell on the poor squirrels, and the magic stopped until Jess and Lily found a way to get the blue dragon to reverse his spell.

Goldie pointed through a gap in the trees. "There's Willowtree River!"

So many animals were crowded at the riverside that the girls could only just see the water, twinkling like a jewel in the sunshine.

"Look!" Goldie pointed her paw. The teams were getting ready by the starting line. The Featherbill duck family chatted beside their pretty blue-and-yellow barge. The Greenhop frog family had brought their widest lily pad, which was the size of Jess's kitchen table at home, and the Flippershell turtles were lining up, too,

each wearing a cap of a different color of the rainbow. Even their rowboat was rainbow-colored!

Jess waved to the Paddlefoot beaver family, who were sitting one behind the other in their orange canoe. On the banks all around, animals were laying out their picnics, and sitting at a judge's table were three elegant swan sisters. Silvia Whitewing, the eldest, nodded gracefully to the girls when they waved.

Then Goldie turned to Jess and Lily. "There's one more thing to do before the race can begin. Come on!"

Emily Prickleback

Jess and Lily followed her downstream along the riverbank to a beautifully polished waterwheel. It turned slowly and steadily as its blades paddled through the water, making a lovely *splish splish* sound.

In front of the waterwheel, a family of hedgehogs were rolling around on the leaves and flowers that littered the riverbank. They spiked the leaves with their prickles, then scurried to shake them off onto a pile, well away from the waterwheel.

One of the smaller hedgehogs scurried over toward the girls.

"It's Harry Prickleback!" said Lily.

"Hello, Jess and Lily," said Harry, as two more adorable little hedgehogs looked curiously at the girls. "This is my brother, Herbie. And this is our little sister, Emily."

Emily was wearing a pretty, sparkly tiara on her head. Lots of leaves and cotton-candy-scented petals were caught in her prickles. "Excuse me," she said, touching Jess's knee. "I like your curly yellow hair."

"Thanks," said Jess. "I like your tiara!"

"Emily won that in a competition," Harry explained proudly. "She had to solve a lot of really hard puzzles."

Lily smiled at Emily. "You must be very smart," she said.

"Oh, yes," said Mr. Prickleback proudly. "Our little Emily is really smart!"

Emily's nose blushed pink.

"Your tiara looks so pretty with the petals on your prickles," said Lily. "We should decorate our hair like that!"

Emily giggled. "It's not decoration," she explained. "It's work. We collect leaves and petals on our prickles so they don't clog up the waterwheel."

Mrs. Prickleback bustled over to help get the leaves off Emily's back. "The Willowtree River flows when we turn the waterwheel," she explained. "We have to make sure it never stops, or the river will disappear."

"Only the Pricklebacks know how to

turn the wheel," Goldie said. "That's why I've come to ask them a favor."

Mr. Prickleback grinned. "Anything for you, Goldie," he said.

"Will you make the river flow a little more quickly, please?" she asked. "We want to give the boats a flying start!"

The younger hedgehogs squealed in delight.

"Of course," said their dad. "Everyone, take your places!"

Lily and Jess grinned at each other happily. They couldn't wait to see the Pricklebacks in action!

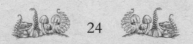

CHAPTER THREE

Unwelcome Visitors

Jess and Lily watched the hedgehogs
waddle over to the waterwheel. Inside it
were five smaller wheels. Each of the
Pricklebacks climbed into one.

"Ready, team?" asked Mr. Prickleback.

"Ready!" they cried.

"Then, one . . . and two . . . and . . .
Ready! Steady! CURL!"

The five hedgehogs immediately curled
up into spiky balls. They rolled forward,
each making their own wheel turn. The
five little wheels each turned a cog that
clicked and clanked, then fit together to
turn the waterwheel. Suddenly, the water
started to rush through it much faster than
before.

"Wow!" said Lily,
as the hedgehogs rolled
so quickly they became
prickly blurs. "No wonder
only the Pricklebacks
can make the
waterwheel work!"
But as the girls
watched the waterwheel
in delight,

Goldie gave a cry. "Oh, no! Girls, look!" she shouted.

A familiar orb of yellow-green light was drifting through the trees, right toward them.

"It's Grizelda!" Jess called to the hedgehogs.

Emily stopped rolling and uncurled. Her little paws flew to her mouth. "The witch!" she squealed.

All the Pricklebacks stopped rolling. They jumped down from the waterwheel and huddled together, their spines quivering with worry.

The orb burst in a shower of fiery

yellow-green sparks. In its place stood a tall, bony woman with green hair swirling around her face like a bunch of snakes. She folded her arms and tapped the sharply pointed toe of one of her high-heeled boots.

"CURL!" Mrs. Prickleback shouted. In a flash, all the hedgehogs rolled themselves into round, prickly balls.

"Your spiky little friends are right to

be afraid," Grizelda sneered. "My next dragon is going to make all the animals leave this forest. Then it will be mine forever! Hahahaa!"

Jess glanced at Lily. Her friend's eyes were wide, but she could tell Lily was determined not to let the witch see that she was scared.

"We're ready for anything your dragon does!" Jess said bravely.

"We'll see about that!" screeched Grizelda. Then, with a snap of her fingers, she disappeared.

Goldie slipped her paws into Jess's and

Lily's hands. "What do you think this dragon will do?" she asked.

They stood, backs together, watching and waiting. But the forest looked just as lovely as before.

The Pricklebacks had just started to uncurl when there was a mighty roar from above.

"Raaargh!"

Circling in the air was Dusty, Grizelda's yellow dragon!

The Pricklebacks seemed to be too frightened to move as the dragon gave a rasping giggle. "Heeheeheeheehee! I'm going to make it lovely and dry," she said. "Friendship Forest will be like a desert!"

Jess was horrified. "You can't do that!" she yelled. "What about the animals?"

"Heeheehee! Who cares about them?" said Dusty. "My yellow scales will look so pretty in the sun!"

Suddenly, she swooped lower.

"Oh, no," cried Jess, "she's heading for the Pricklebacks!"

"Run!" shouted Lily.

"Hide!" yelled Goldie and Jess together.

But the Pricklebacks didn't move. They shook with fright, their spines quivering.

Dusty flew toward them. She gave another sandy roar and chanted:

"Magic make these hedgehogs change
So they all turn to stone.
Then the river will flow no more,
But be as dry as bone."

 33

Lily, Jess, and Goldie watched in horror as the hedgehogs' brown prickles turned gray. Finally, their trembling paws turned gray and were still.

Jess ran to pick up Harry. His spines were cold and hard, and he didn't feel like a real hedgehog at all. She clutched him to her and turned to Lily and Goldie. Her face was pale.

"Oh, no!" she gasped. "The poor Pricklebacks. Grizelda's dragon has turned them to stone!"

CHAPTER FOUR

A Threat to Willowtree River

With a grinding noise, the waterwheel slowed to a stop.

The yellow dragon flew away, giggling to herself. "Heeheehee! Now the forest will be dry and lovely, just right for sunbathing!"

 35

Goldie and Lily rushed over to the stone hedgehogs.

"Maybe they just need waking up," Lily said desperately.

Jess looked at Herbie. His black beady eyes were open wide, and his little nose was frozen in the air. "Herbie?" she called, but the hedgehog didn't move.

"It's no good," Goldie said finally. "We can't break dragon magic, remember? Dragons have to reverse their spells themselves."

Jess was close to tears. "But we can't

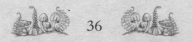

36

leave them like this," she said, "just four

tiny hedgehog statues."

Lily gasped. "Four!" she repeated.

"There are only four of them."

Goldie grasped Lily's hands. "You're

right!" she said.

Jess was puzzled. "What do you mean?"

Then she realized. "Of course—there

should be five! Where is little Emily

Prickleback?"

As they looked around, they heard a faint squeak. Then a little pile of leaves and petals started to uncurl, and a tiny, snuffly face peeked out.

"Emily!" cried Lily. "You had so many petals stuck on your prickles that Dusty didn't spot you."

She picked up the trembling creature, who snuggled into the crook of her elbow.

38

"What about my family?" Emily asked tearfully.

Jess stroked her cheek with a finger. "Don't you worry," she said softly. "We figured out how to get Chilly the ice dragon to reverse his magic. We'll find out how to make Dusty end hers, too."

Emily blinked back tears and clenched her little paws. "Mom and Dad say I'm good at figuring things out," she said, "so I'll help!"

Leaving the statues behind, they hurried back up the river, where they found the animals clustered near the starting

line, still waiting for the river to speed up
so the race could begin. The Featherbill
family had started a water balloon fight
and the ducklings were all waddling
around, chasing one another with colorful
water balloons. Ellie Featherbill squealed
in delight as a balloon burst all over her
fluffy feathers.

"Look," Mrs. Featherbill cried. "The girls and Goldie are back!"

Goldie quickly explained what had happened. Everyone started chattering with worry.

Agatha Glitterwing the magpie put a comforting wing around Emily. "We can't have the race now," she said. "Not while the poor Pricklebacks are under a spell!"

Lily was staring at the river. Something about it didn't look the same. "Does the river look shallower to you?" she asked Jess anxiously.

Emily raced to the riverside. "The waterwheel must be stopping. The river's not just slowing down, it's disappearing!"

Goldie's whiskers quivered with worry. "We need to save Emily's family so they can get it turning again. If we don't, the river will turn as dry as bone, just like Dusty said in her spell!"

The Greenhops hopped up and down in a panic, croaking, "No Willowtree River? What will we do?"

"Oh, my!" squawked Agatha. "All the trees and flowers will die, and we'll have nothing to drink!"

"We'll have to leave Friendship Forest!" cried Mr. Silverback the badger.

"That's exactly what Grizelda wants," Jess said. "Did anyone notice which way Dusty went?"

"She was going to sunbathe," said little Emily. "Maybe she went to the beach?"

Lily smiled at the hedgehog. "Great idea, Emily! Your brothers were right— you really are smart."

Emily's nose turned pink again.

"Coral Cove is close to here," said Goldie. "It's a little sandy beach where Willowtree River turns a corner. We just

need to follow the
river. Come on, let's
see if Dusty's there!"

Emily rode in Jess's
pocket, being careful
not to prick her with
her spines, as the
three friends set off.

"Good luck!" cried the Twinkletails.

"Take care," called Mr. Silverback.

"Don't worry!" Goldie shouted back.
"We'll save the Pricklebacks!"

Jess nodded. "After all, we've got a very
smart hedgehog to help us . . ."

CHAPTER FIVE

Kingfishers in Trouble

The group of friends hurried past trees and
bushes. Emily peeked out of Jess's pocket,
holding her tiara in place with one paw.

Soon the bushes got so thick that
they couldn't see the river at all. As they
walked along, they heard a funny noise.
"Chee-kee, chee-kee!"

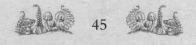

"It must be a bird," Lily said, thinking about the birds they sometimes helped at the wildlife hospital. "It sounds upset."

They pushed through the thick bushes to the river. As they got closer, they heard more and more bird voices crying out. "Chee-kee! Chee-kee!" they squawked.

When they reached the river, everyone gasped. The water had almost completely

disappeared, leaving only a muddy ditch behind. And stuck in the mud were five small birds! Their feathers were plastered with mud, leaves, and bits of twigs.

"It's the Blueflash kingfisher family," Goldie cried, running to them. "What happened?"

"Chee-kee! Chee-kee!" Mrs. Blueflash cheeped, ruffling her feathers with worry.

"Oh, Goldie! We stopped for a dip on our way to the Rushy River Race, so our colors would look fresh and bright. But now our wings are covered in thick mud so we can't fly!"

One of the little Blueflashes flapped his wings, but he couldn't take off. "We'll never get home again," he said sadly. "It's too far to hop."

"Don't worry, we'll help you," said Lily. "There must be a way we can clean your feathers."

"Lily and Jess help any animals in need," Goldie said comfortingly.

"But how?" Lily whispered anxiously. "There's no water to wash them."

"Oh!" squeaked Emily. "I know how— I have an idea!" She wriggled out of Jess's pocket and hopped down onto the ground. "Come here," Emily called to the Blueflash family. One by one the kingfishers hopped out of the ditch, looking bedraggled and sorry for themselves.

"Just copy me!" Emily showed them how to roll around on the ground just like hedgehogs. "The mud on your feathers has dried in the sunshine," she explained, "so if you roll, it will rub off!"

"It's a dust bath!" Jess giggled in delight.

The Blueflashes did as Emily said, and once they saw that her plan was working, they all cheered up.

The young Blueflashes giggled as they rolled. Soon their brilliant blue-and-orange feathers were clean. They fluffed

them up, then the kingfishers flapped their
wings and took off, whizzing back and
forth in delight.

"They're so fast that all I can see are
blue flashes!" Lily said, laughing.

"Great job, Emily!" said Jess. "That
was really smart."

Goldie told Mr. and Mrs. Blueflash

about the spell Dusty had put on the rest of the Prickleback family.

"The beach is still very far away," Mrs. Blueflash told them. "But we'll see if she's there. We can be there and back in a flash."

"Thank you!" Jess called.

The kingfisher family took off in a blur of color. Minutes later they were back, shaking their heads. "She's not there," Mrs. Blueflash told them.

"We'll keep an eye out for her," promised Mr. Blueflash. "We really need the river back."

One of the youngsters fluttered past them. "I'm cold," he said. "Let's fly up higher, where the air is warmer!"

"Wait a minute! Could that be where Dusty is?" Lily wondered out loud. "She's not at the beach, but could she be sunbathing high in the treetops?"

Jess nodded. "It's worth a try."

Goldie's whiskers twitched. "But there are so many trees," she pointed out. "How do we know where she'd be?"

"Oh, I know!" said Emily. "She'd be up the tallest tree in the forest. That's the Treasure Tree!"

"Of course!" said Jess, remembering that they'd climbed the tree on one of their adventures. "Your family is lucky you're so smart, Emily. We'll track Dusty down in no time. Let's go!"

CHAPTER SIX

A Cleverfeather Invention!

The Treasure Tree towered above them, its leaves shimmering in the sunlight. There were all sorts of colorful fruits and nuts growing along its branches. Normally, it was busy with animals gathering food, but today everyone was at the river and the Treasure Tree was deserted.

Jess peered into the branches. Was Dusty up there somewhere, sunning herself on the highest branch? Magical vines hung around the trunk to help animals climb the tree safely. Jess ran to grab one but almost fell when she stubbed her foot on something hard.

It was a grapefruit, but it was made of stone!

"Dusty must have done this!" she cried, showing the others. "She's definitely here!"

"Goodness," said a voice nearby. "A

pone stair—I mean a stone pear! This isn't right. Not right at all!"

Jess grinned. She knew that voice. It was Mr. Cleverfeather the owl. Sure enough, when they looked behind the broad tree trunk, there he was with one of his inventions.

"Goldie!" he cried. "And Less and Jilly—I mean, Jess and Lily. Oh, dear, I do get my words muddled. Are you picking fruit? Would you like to borrow my invention? It's a ticking pool."

"A ticking pool?" said Emily, peeping out from Jess's pocket.

"He means a picking tool." Lily giggled. She jumped back as a stone coconut hit the ground with a thump.

Jess told Mr. Cleverfeather about Dusty. "So you see," she finished, "we have to get her to take the spell off the other Pricklebacks. If we don't, Willowtree River will be gone forever."

"There!" whispered Lily excitedly.

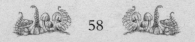

"To the left of those bananas, above the coconuts. It's Dusty's tail!"

Sure enough, there was a yellow tail swinging lazily back and forth.

"Watch out!" cried Emily. "Pineapple!"

They leaped aside as a stone pineapple smashed through the branches, hitting the ground with a thud and shattering into tiny pieces.

There was a giggle from above. "Heeheehee!"

"Dusty must think it's funny to turn fruit to stone while she sunbathes," Jess said angrily.

"Look out!" said Goldie, dodging

as a stone walnut fell from the tree.

"Now that we've dotted Spusty—I mean,

spotted Dusty," said Mr. Cleverfeather,

"we must think of a way to get her down."

"If we can't," Emily said anxiously,

"we'll never get her to reverse that spell."

They all thought hard.

"If only Dusty knew how much fun

water could be," Lily
said, thinking about the
Rushy River Race and the
lovely day they had planned.

Emily looked thoughtful. "It's like
a puzzle," she said. "There must be
something we can do . . ." Suddenly, she
gave an excited squeak. "I know! Do you
remember what the Featherbills were
doing while everyone was waiting
for the race to start?"

A grin spread over Jess's face as she realized what Emily meant. "They were having a water balloon fight!" she said.

"Emily, that's so smart!" said Lily. "Everyone loves water balloon fights."

"Even dragons?" Jess asked.

"Let's hope so," Goldie said, crossing her paws tightly.

Every inch of Mr. Cleverfeather's inventing shed was crammed with tools and gadgets. Lily, Jess, Goldie, and Emily peered around curiously. Jess grinned as she looked at the plans for a Cake

Creator, which were spread out on the wise old owl's desk.

"My next invention," said Mr. Cleverfeather, sweeping the plans aside. "But that's not what knee weed. I mean, we need." He rummaged around. "Banana peeler for the parrots . . . no. Automatic ear wash for rabbits . . . no. Ah!" he cried. "Here we are." He opened a large box.

Jess and Lily peered into it. "Water balloons!" they cried.

Mr. Cleverfeather chuckled. "Ah, these aren't ordinary balloons," he said.

"They're Hi-Soak Balloons, just like
the ones the Featherbills were using. I
invented them so we could all have water
fights on hot days. What fun!"

"Perfect," said Goldie. "Hopefully,
Dusty will think it's fun, too."

Mr. Cleverfeather passed Jess a full
watering can. Lily held a red balloon
steady while Jess filled it. Then she knotted
it and batted it into the air with her hand.

"Catch, Emily!" she said.

The little hedgehog tried to catch it, but
she missed, and it landed on her prickly
head and burst.

Pop!

It showered
her with
water.

Splosh!

Emily fell
backward in

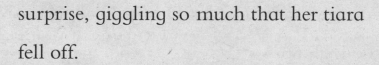

surprise, giggling so much that her tiara
fell off.

Jess helped Emily to her feet. "But
how will we fill up the balloons?" she
wondered. "The river's gone."

"There's just enough water in the
watering can to fill these ones," said Lily.

"And if our plan works, we'll get the river back soon!"

While Mr. Cleverfeather, Jess, and Goldie filled as many balloons as they could, Lily used her skirt to pat Emily dry, then popped her back in Jess's pocket.

"Just one more thing," said Lily, "how can we throw them at Dusty? She's much too high up."

"Don't worry," said Goldie. "I'm sure our bird friends will help us make a very soggy delivery—of Hi-Soak Balloons!"

CHAPTER SEVEN

Attack!

Captain Ace flew above the treetops,
towing his beautiful patchwork hot air
balloon through the sky behind him.

Lily, Jess, and Goldie were inside the
basket hanging beneath the balloon, with
a huge pile of filled water balloons at their
feet. Emily perched on the side of the basket,

with Lily's arm
around her to stop
her from falling off.
Captain Ace
pulled on a rope.
Puff! Puff! Puff!
Bubbles streamed up
into the balloon. Then they burst,
filling it with hot air.

Lily looked to the left and waved to
Mrs. Taptree the woodpecker and her

chicks, Dig and Tipper, who were flying alongside.

They gave muffled chirps. "Quick! Quick!"

Jess waved to the Blueflash family, who called, "Chee-kee! Chee-kee!" Their voices were muffled, too, because each bird had a bunch of water balloons dangling from its beak. Even tiny Jenny Littlefeather the wren was carrying one. Her wings beat twice as fast as the other birds' as she struggled to keep up.

Lily tightened her arm around Emily

and said to Jess, "Aren't we lucky to have so many wonderful friends?"

Jess nodded happily. "Look!" she cried, as they drew near the Treasure Tree. "There's Dusty!"

The dragon was lying on her back on the highest branch, her eyes closed and her wings outspread.

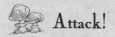

"Captain Ace," whispered Goldie, "can we go a little closer?"

The stork nodded.

They drifted along in silence. The birds flew as quietly as they could, and Lily and Jess held their breath. If Dusty saw them before they could convince her to play, she could turn them to stone, too, and they'd drop out of the sky!

Suddenly, the shadow of the hot air balloon fell on the dragon . . . and she opened her eyes.

"Oh, no," gasped Jess. "She's seen us!"

Scrambling to her feet, Dusty let out a huge roar. "Raaargh!"

"Look out, Ace!" yelled Lily.

Ace flapped his wings hard, yanking the hot air balloon away from Dusty's roar. Lily and Jess could feel the blast of her hot breath just missing the basket. The balloon rocked from side to side, sending the girls and Goldie toppling backward in the basket.

"Hold on, Emily!" yelled Lily.

The little hedgehog was clinging onto the edge. But as the basket swayed, her paws slipped—and she fell over the side!

"Emily!"

Lily cried.

Lily and Jess
leaned out, expecting to see
the little hedgehog crashing
through the branches below.

Instead, a terrified
little face looked up at
them from the edge of the
basket. Two paws clung tightly to a
knotted rope.

Jess leaned over and scooped up Emily.
"You're safe now," she said, cuddling her
closely. Emily's prickles were standing on

end with fright, but Jess didn't mind being spiked. "Are you all right, Emily?"

"I'm okay," Emily said, shakily.

The balloon drifted back toward the dragon, just out of reach of her hot, sandy breath.

"Dusty!" called Goldie. "We've come to ask you something—"

"Pah!" interrupted the dragon. "Go away! Can't you see I'm busy sunning my pretty scales?" She lay down to sunbathe again.

"I think it's time to try our plan," whispered Lily. She called, "Dusty! Do

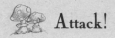

you want to find out how much fun
water can be?"

Dusty gave a growl. "Getting wet is
NOT fun! My scales are only pretty
when they're shining in the sun!" she
snarled angrily. She beat her wings
and took off, flying toward them, her
mouth open.

"She's going to get us!" yelled Jess.
"Quick, everyone . . . Fire!"

Lily and Jess grabbed balloons in both
hands and threw them at the dragon.
Splat! Splosh!

"Raaaaargh!" roared Dusty, flapping

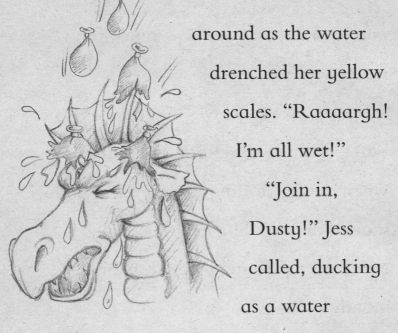

around as the water
drenched her yellow
scales. "Raaaargh!
I'm all wet!"

"Join in,
Dusty!" Jess
called, ducking
as a water

balloon sped over her head. "Missed me!"
she laughed.

The birds carefully swooped down and
put a pile of water balloons next to Dusty.

Dusty picked up a wobbly water
balloon in her claws. Lily and Jess held

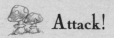

their breath. Had it worked, or had they made the yellow dragon even angrier?

Splosh! Splat! Splosh! Water balloons were flying everywhere.

One of the balloons burst over Dusty's head. Without thinking, the dragon threw the balloon at one of the woodpecker chicks, who burst out laughing as the water hit his feathers.

"Raaaa . . . heeheehee!" Dusty said, her roar becoming a giggle. Her scaly yellow face was surprised. "That feels funny!"

"It's working!" cried Goldie. "Dusty! Are you having fun?"

"Heeheehee!" chuckled the dragon, throwing a balloon at Goldie. Goldie giggled as it burst on her tail.

Dusty flew up into the sky, dodging and diving and throwing water balloons everywhere. Finally, the dripping dragon landed back on the highest branch of the Treasure Tree. "More! More!" she cried.

Lily looked around. But everyone had used up all their balloons.

"We've
run out of
balloons,
Dusty," Lily
called. "And
we can't fill up any
more because the river is all
dried up."

Dusty looked upset. "But I want to
keep on playing," she grumbled, her tail
drooping.

"So do we," Jess told her. "But we need
the river back first. Will you lift your spell

from the Pricklebacks so they can make it flow again?"

Dusty flew around in a loop-the-loop. "Yes," she agreed, "I will! Then we can play again!"

There was a chorus of happy cheeps, chirps, and squawks from the birds. Captain Ace did a loop-the-loop, and the girls, Emily, and Goldie gave a big cheer.

"Hooray!" cried Emily, her eyes shining. "We did it!"

CHAPTER EIGHT

The Rushy River Race

Captain Ace towed his hot air balloon, with its happy passengers, back to the waterwheel. Dusty flew beside them, giggling as water droplets shimmered on her scales. "My scales look even prettier," she boasted. "The water makes them sparkle even more than the sunshine!"

The balloon drifted over the muddy ditch where the river should have been.

Captain Ace looked back. "Prepare for landing," he mumbled, with the rope still in his beak.

A few moments later, they were down. The birds landed next to the waterwheel and the girls, Goldie, and Emily climbed out of the basket. Dusty skidded to a stop beside them.

Emily ran to her family and hugged the cold little stone figures. "You'll be

back to normal soon," she said. "I

promise!"

"Dusty's going to reverse the spell

now," said Goldie. "Stand back, Emily!"

Dusty stood in front of the stone

hedgehogs and chanted:

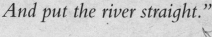

> *"Dragon wings stop Dusty's spell,*
>
> *Getting wet is great.*
>
> *Make hedgehogs be themselves again,*
>
> *And put the river straight."*

The Pricklebacks started to turn from gray into their usual colors. They looked around in surprise.

Harry rubbed dust from his eyes. "What a weird dream I had," he said.

"Me, too," said Herbie.

"The dragon!" shouted Mrs. Prickleback when she saw Dusty. "Where's Emily?"

"I'm here!" Emily cried, as Jess set her

down. She ran to hug and kiss her family.

"You were made of stone!" Emily said,
and she told her family everything that
had happened.

"We couldn't have saved you without
Emily," added Jess. "She's so clever!"

Emily's nose turned extra pink as her
family hugged her again.

Mr. Prickleback gasped. He pointed at
the muddy ditch where Willowtree River
was supposed to be flowing. "Oh, my
prickles!" he cried. "The river is gone!"

Mrs. Prickleback began hurrying
toward the waterwheel. "The waterwheel

has stopped! We have to get it turning again. Hurry, everyone!"

The whole hedgehog family scrambled into their little wheels.

"Ready, team?" asked Mr. Prickleback.

"Ready!" they cried.

"CURL!" Mr. Prickleback shouted.

The Pricklebacks curled up and began rolling. The waterwheel groaned, then it started to turn. Immediately, a trickle of water flowed through the riverbed. Lily and Jess gasped in delight as the trickle grew bigger and bigger, the water swirling along until Willowtree River was back to normal. All the watching animals cheered as the Pricklebacks came out of the waterwheel and had a family hug.

"I'm c–c–c–cold," said a voice.

The girls turned to see Dusty. She was shivering.

"It looks like you need to get dry again after the water fight," said Jess.

Mrs. Prickleback hurried inside and came out with towels for them all. But the dragon was still shivering miserably.

"I-I-I-I'm going to s–s–s–s–sunbathe," she said, her teeth chattering.

"Dusty can't go back to the Treasure Tree," Goldie whispered in alarm. "What if she turns more fruit into stone?"

"What about Coral Cove?" Lily said. "Wouldn't that be a nice place for Dusty to sunbathe, away from all the animals?"

"We know the perfect place for you to sunbathe, Dusty," Jess told her.

Dusty gave a little smile.

"It's by the river, so you can play in the

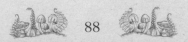

water and then get dry again whenever you like," Jess continued.

"We can have another water balloon fight tomorrow!" Emily suggested. "And you can have some of my petals to decorate your scales."

"If you promise not to cause any more trouble," Goldie said firmly.

Dusty's smile turned into a wide grin. She whizzed around them in a happy circle. "I promise! Heeheehee! I'm going to have so much fun!"

They told Dusty where Coral Cove was. She flapped away, giggling.

"I'm glad she's happy," said Lily.

Just then they heard an excited squeal from nearby. All the other creatures were happy, too—with the river back to normal, the race could finally begin!

Jess and Lily jumped up and down as all the boats raced down the river as fast as they could. The Pricklebacks had turned the waterwheel so much that the river was gushing and rushing. As they cheered, two boats inched ahead of the others. Everyone shouted loudly for their favorite team.

"Go, go, Greenhops!"

"Faster, faster, Flippershells!"

It was going to be a close finish. The Greenhops' lily pad and the Paddlefoots' canoe were neck and neck as they sped toward the finish line.

Everyone turned to look at the judges excitedly. The swans whispered to one another and everyone in the crowd held their breath.

"Tie!" called Silvia Whitewing. "I declare you both winners!"

With the race over, all the animals spread out blankets and unpacked their picnics. Everyone was excited, and plenty of food-swapping went on. Mrs. Twinkletail had brought enough hazelnut chips for half the animals in the forest!

All too soon it was time for the girls to leave. "Thank you!" the animals called as they said good-bye. Emily gave them a special hug before rolling off to play with her brothers.

Goldie took Jess and Lily to the Friendship Tree. She touched the trunk with her paw, and the magical door appeared.

"Thank you for helping us again," she

said. "Grizelda has two more dragons, though. She's bound to think up another wicked plan soon."

"Don't worry, we'll be ready," said Lily.

"Just come and get us," Jess added. "We can't wait to see you again, Goldie!"

They hugged their friend good-bye and stepped into the

94

golden light that shimmered inside
the tree. As the glow faded, they found
themselves back in Brightley Meadow.
As usual, no time at all had passed while
they were in Friendship Forest and it was
still a misty morning. They had a whole
day of fun at Helping Paw to come!

"What a wonderful adventure!" cried
Lily as they held hands and ran back
toward the wildlife hospital.

They slowed down as they reached
the barn.

The woman with the hedgehog was
walking to her car.

"She must be so glad to have her pet back!" Jess said.

"I bet he's just as clever as another little hedgehog we know!" Lily said. "I can't wait to see Emily Prickleback and her family again!"

"Me, either!" said Jess.

The End

Grizelda's next dragon wants to make the forest inky dark! Find out if Lily, Jess, and Goldie can stop him in their next adventure,

Ruby Fuzzybrush's
Star Dance

Turn the page for a sneak peek . . .

The foxes stepped, dipped, glided, and turned around the moonstone, weaving complicated patterns. Each time they swept past one another and their bushy tails touched, the glow from the moonstone grew brighter.

Lily glanced up at the night sky. "Look, Jess!" she whispered. "The stars are coming out."

Jess gazed at the sky. "It's so beautiful!" she cried. "Oh! The brighter the moonstone gets, the more stars appear."

The girls stared in delight as hundreds— no, thousands—of stars winked and blinked in the darkness. Soon it was almost as bright as daytime, and the forest was lit up with sparkling silver starlight.

Suddenly, Rusty cried out, "Look, Mom, Dad! Up there in the sky!"

Read

Ruby Fuzzybrush's Star Dance

to find out what happens next!

Puzzle Fun!

Can you help Emily find the following words
in this magical word search?

U	B	Y	X	Z	A	M	S	A	R
S	W	F	O	R	E	S	T	G	A
E	O	F	C	V	N	E	Y	R	H
F	I	Z	V	M	W	Z	R	I	G
L	U	Q	W	A	W	J	E	Z	W
W	S	S	Y	G	I	U	M	E	I
S	P	E	W	O	U	L	I	L	Y
S	H	C	E	P	A	P	Q	D	P
E	J	E	B	T	I	A	R	A	T
J	R	L	I	L	G	R	Z	M	P

WORDS TO FIND:

Tiara
Forest
Grizelda
Lily
Jess

ANSWERS

J	R	L	I	L	G	R	Z	M	P
E	J	E	B	T	I	A	R	A	T
S	H	C	E	P	A	P	Q	D	P
S	P	E	W	O	U	L	I	L	Y
W	S	S	Y	G	I	U	M	E	I
L	U	Q	W	A	W	J	E	Z	W
F	I	Z	V	M	W	Z	R	I	G
E	O	F	C	V	N	E	Y	R	H
S	W	F	O	R	E	S	T	G	A
U	B	Y	X	Z	A	M	S	A	R

Lily and Jess's Animal Facts

Lily and Jess love lots of different animals—both in Friendship Forest and in the real world.

Here are their top facts about . . .

HEDGEHOGS

like Emily Prickleback.

• Hedgehogs are nocturnal animals, which means they like to sleep during the day.

• Hedgehogs like to eat beetles, millipedes, worms, slugs, and snails.

• Baby hedgehogs are sometimes called "urchins."

• Lots of people think that hedgehogs like to eat milk and bread, but actually, canned dog or cat food is healthier for them.

RAINBOW magic™

Which Magical Fairies Have You Met?

- ❑ The Rainbow Fairies
- ❑ The Weather Fairies
- ❑ The Jewel Fairies
- ❑ The Pet Fairies
- ❑ The Dance Fairies
- ❑ The Music Fairies
- ❑ The Sports Fairies
- ❑ The Party Fairies
- ❑ The Ocean Fairies
- ❑ The Night Fairies
- ❑ The Magical Animal Fairies
- ❑ The Princess Fairies
- ❑ The Superstar Fairies
- ❑ The Fashion Fairies
- ❑ The Sugar & Spice Fairies
- ❑ The Earth Fairies
- ❑ The Magical Crafts Fairies
- ❑ The Baby Animal Rescue Fairies
- ❑ The Fairy Tale Fairies

📖 SCHOLASTIC

Find all of your favorite fairy friends at
scholastic.com/rainbowmagic

RMFAIRY13

SPECIAL EDITION

Which Magical Fairies Have You Met?

- ❑ Joy the Summer Vacation Fairy
- ❑ Holly the Christmas Fairy
- ❑ Kylie the Carnival Fairy
- ❑ Stella the Star Fairy
- ❑ Shannon the Ocean Fairy
- ❑ Trixie the Halloween Fairy
- ❑ Gabriella the Snow Kingdom Fairy
- ❑ Juliet the Valentine Fairy
- ❑ Mia the Bridesmaid Fairy
- ❑ Flora the Dress-Up Fairy
- ❑ Paige the Christmas Play Fairy
- ❑ Emma the Easter Fairy
- ❑ Cara the Camp Fairy
- ❑ Destiny the Rock Star Fairy
- ❑ Belle the Birthday Fairy

- ❑ Olympia the Games Fairy
- ❑ Selena the Sleepover Fairy
- ❑ Cheryl the Christmas Tree Fairy
- ❑ Florence the Friendship Fairy
- ❑ Lindsay the Luck Fairy
- ❑ Brianna the Tooth Fairy
- ❑ Autumn the Falling Leaves Fairy
- ❑ Keira the Movie Star Fairy
- ❑ Addison the April Fool's Day Fairy
- ❑ Bailey the Babysitter Fairy
- ❑ Natalie the Christmas Stocking Fairy
- ❑ Lila and Myla the Twins Fairies
- ❑ Chelsea the Congratulations Fairy
- ❑ Carly the School Fairy
- ❑ Angelica the Angel Fairy
- ❑ Blossom the Flower Girl Fairy

3 stories in each one!

▌SCHOLASTIC

Find all of your favorite fairy friends at
scholastic.com/rainbowmagic

HIT entertainment

RMSPECIAL17

Visit Friendship Forest, where animals can talk and magic exists!

Meet best friends Jess and Lily and their adorable animal pals in this enchanting series from the creator of Rainbow Magic!

SCHOLASTIC

scholastic.com

MAGICAF2